P9-DUE-413

Jamal's Journey

WITHDRAWN

Michael Foreman

Andersen Press USA

Walk, walk, walk. That's what camels do.

It's all right for Jamal's mama and baba, they've got long legs.
He has little legs, so it's hard for him to keep up.
The people have little legs too, especially the boy,
but most of the time they don't walk. They ride.

Jamal looks at the falcons. They are lucky too—
the birds get carried everywhere, except when they soar
through the sky, hunting the small creatures of the desert.
But Jamal is a little camel, and camels have to walk, walk, walk.

Suddenly there is a roaring noise.

Jamal doesn't know what is happening, there is sand everywhere,

whooshing and whirling in the wild wind!

Sand in his eyes. Sand in
his nose. Sand in his ears.

"Mama! Baba!"
cries Jamal.

Now there is sand
in his mouth.

He turns his back to the howling wind,
making himself as small as possible.

The wind roars louder and louder,
thundering around him.
Then it stops as suddenly as it started.
The sand-filled sky has transformed
into a sky of stars.

"Mama! Baba!
Where are you?"

Jamal looks for footprints by the light of the moon,
but everything has been blown away by the wind.
Which way to go? With no clues,
Jamal just follows the moonlight.

Finally, dawn breaks across the empty land of sand.

But it is not quite empty—
a tiny head with twitching
ears is looking at Jamal.

It is a jerboa!

Now a spiky monitor lizard
peeps out from under a
rock and a big brown hare
bounces over the hill.

"Hello!" cries Jamal to them all.
"I am lost. Can you help me?"

But suddenly the tiny jerboa
sees the lizard and jumps
back into her hole.

Then the lizard feels the vibrations as the big brown hare
hops closer and dives back under his rock.

A moment later, the big brown hare twitches his huge ears,
looks up at the sky, and races away, leaving Jamal alone again.

The lizard frightened the jerboa.
The hare frightened the lizard.
But what frightened the hare?

Jamal looks up to the sky and spots a tiny dot,
high in the blue, spiraling toward him.

It's a falcon, like the ones
who ride on Mama and Baba.

She hovers in front of Jamal
and then flies in a big loop.

As the little camel walks toward the falcon, it flies
a little further away and loops again. Jamal smiles.

Jamal follows the falcon as it circles
through the sky toward distant dunes. It's
hot work climbing hills with his little legs.

"Oh!" cries Jamal. "I can see
a great city, far away, and
beyond that, the shining sea!"

The falcon zooms off toward a cloud of dust that is moving slowly across the sandy plain. Jamal gallops after her.

In a short time, she is whirling and looping
in the air with the other falcons. And the
dust cloud has turned toward them too.

"Mama! Baba!" Jamal cries. But ahead of them all is
the boy. He is racing across the sand to hug his friend.

Together they all set off toward the faraway city. Jamal stays close to Mama and Baba, and the boy walks beside him: he doesn't want his camel to get lost ever again.

Jamal had never been in a city before. It is so busy, so noisy—the market, the boats, the sea. So exciting!

Now Jamal knows the world is more than just sand.
When his legs are long and strong, he wants to see it all.

One day, the boy will ride on him. And
Jamal will walk, walk, walk, far and wide, from
gleaming cities to shining seas.

And he will always take his friendly falcon
along, just in case they get lost.